Diplodocus
dip-lod-oh-kus

Oviraptor
oh-vee-rap-tor

Pteranodon
ter-an-oh-don

Stegosaurus
steg-oh-sore-us

Tyrannosaurus
tie-ran-oh-sore-us

For Peter —M. M.

For Henry, Elinor, Ollie, and Milly —A. A.

Originally published in Great Britain by Orchard Books, a division of Hachette Children's Books, in 2010
First published in the United States of America in November 2010
by Walker Publishing Company, Inc., a division of Bloomsbury Publishing, Inc.
www.bloomsburykids.com

For information about permission to reproduce selections from this book, write to
Permissions, Walker BFYR, 175 Fifth Avenue, New York, New York 10010

Library of Congress Cataloging-in-Publication Data
available upon request
ISBN 978-0-8027-2195-2 (hardcover) • ISBN 978-0-8027-2196-9 (reinforced)

Art created with cut-paper collage; typeset in Billy Bold

Printed in China by WKT Company Ltd., Shenzhen, Guangdong
1 3 5 7 9 10 8 6 4 2 (hardcover)
1 3 5 7 9 10 8 6 4 2 (reinforced)

All papers used by Bloomsbury Publishing, Inc., are natural, recyclable products
made from wood grown in well-managed forests. The manufacturing processes
conform to the environmental regulations of the country of origin.

Margaret Mayo illustrated by Alex Ayliffe

STOMP, DINOSAUR, STOMP!

Walker & Company New York

Mighty Tyrannosaurus

loved stomp, **stomp, stomping,**
gigantic legs **striding,** enormous jaws **opening,**

jagged teeth waiting for guzzle, **guzzling!**

So **stomp,** Tyrannosaurus, **stomp!**

Immense Diplodocus

loved swish, swish, swishing,

long tail **flicking** and fast whip, whipping,

enemy **surprising** and—*smack!*—scaring.

So **swish**, Diplodocus, **swish!**

Crested Pteranodon

loved glide, glide, gliding,
spreading wide wings, circling, rising,

higher and higher, **swooping** and **soaring.**

So **glide**, Pteranodon, **glide!**

Fierce Velociraptor

loved hunt, **hunt, hunting,**

in fearsome packs **running, racing,**

hooked claws ready for quick **pouncing.**

So **hunt,** Velociraptor, **hunt!**

Sleek Plesiosaurus

loved zoom, zoom, zooming,
sturdy paddles swooshing, **flapping,**

neck lunging, teeth showing—**snatch!**—fish **trapping.**

So **zoom,** Plesiosaurus, **zoom!**

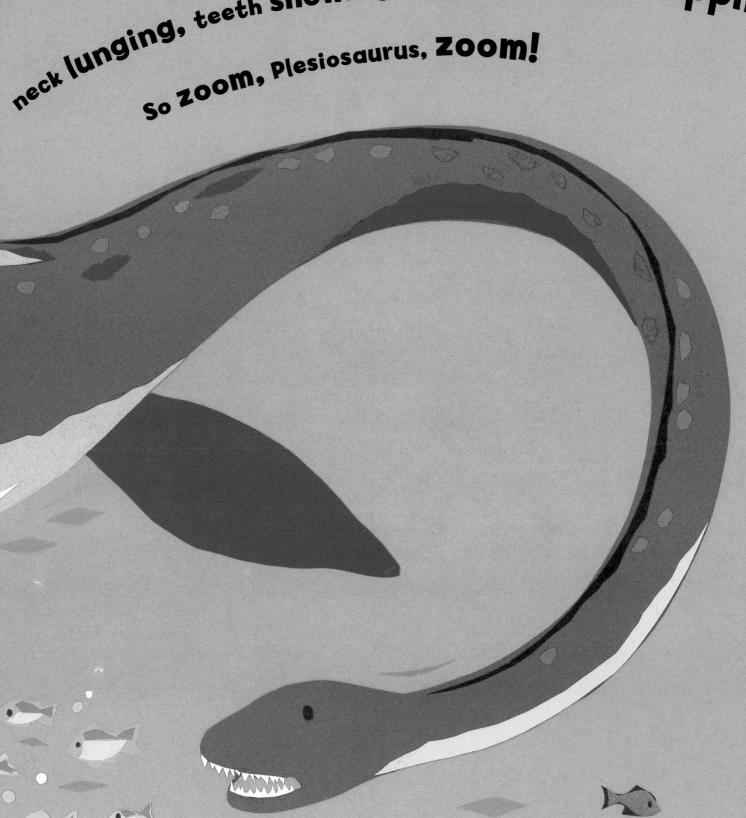

Tough Ankylosaurus

loved whack, **whack, whacking,**

tail-club **swinging,** battles **winning,**

while hiding safely under spikes and armor plating.

So whack, Ankylosaurus, whack!

Massive Brachiosaurus

loved gulp, gulp, gulping,

leaves **picking,** mouth **stuffing** . . . no **chewing!**

Fast **eating,** hungry, hungry giant . . . more food needing.

So **gulp,** Brachiosaurus, **gulp!**

Wrinkly Triceratops

loved charge, **charge, charging,**

thumpety-thump! Huge feet **pounding,**

horns **jutting**, and—_wham!_—head-butting.

So **charge**, Triceratops, **charge!**

Stiff-tailed Iguanodon

loved chomp, **chomp, chomping,**

tough plants **grabbing, cutting,** and **biting,**

chewing, mashing, and noisy **grinding.**

So **chomp,** Iguanodon, **chomp!**

Feathered Oviraptor

loved guard, **guard**, **guarding**,

soft sand **shaping**, snug nest **making**,

eggs protecting, until—cric-crac!—babies hatching.

So guard, Oviraptor, guard!

Fantastic Stegosaurus

loved stroll, **stroll, strolling,**

tiny eyes **glaring,** spiky tail **waving,**

showing off big curvy plates . . . and looking quite amazing!

So stroll, Stegosaurus, stroll!

Imagine the creatures in a grand parade—

with no fighting allowed and no one afraid!

Some **plodding,** some **swooping,** while others just **romp,**

and Tyrannosaurus leading . . .

STOMP! STOMP! STOMP!

Ankylosaurus
an-ki-loh-sore-us

Iguanodon
ig-wah-noh-don

Triceratops
try-seh-ra-tops

Brachiosaurus
brak-ee-oh-sore-us

Velociraptor
vel-oss-uh-rap-tor

Plesiosaurus
plee-see-oh-sore-us